DESTROY THE LIQUIDATOR

#4
DESTROY THE LIQUIDATOR

RYDER WINDHAM

SCHOLASTIC INC.
New York Toronto London Auckland Sydney

ISBN 0-590-12796-9

12 11 10 9 8 7 6 5 4 3 2 1   7 8 9/9 0 1 2/0

Printed in the U.S.A.

First Scholastic printing, December 1997

DESTROY THE LIQUIDATOR

PRELIMINARY MISSION

CHAPTER ONE

The Imperial Star Destroyer *Liquidator* exited hyperspace and entered the Yavin system. Admiral Termo stood on the bridge, gazing out the main viewport as the stars came into focus.

Seeing nothing but clear starfields, Termo realized that the Death Star truly had been obliterated. There wasn't even any sign of floating wreckage.

Termo was the only person aboard the *Liquidator* who knew of the Death Star's destruction. He assumed the Emperor wanted to delay the news so the galaxy would not immediately know of the Empire's loss. Termo allowed the *Liquidator*'s crew to believe the Death Star still existed.

But the crew was uneasy. They knew the Death Star had failed to meet them in the Delrakkin system. Furthermore, the *Liquidator* had suffered great losses in the battle at Delrakkin. Numerous TIE fighters and twenty-three Imperial-owned X-wing starfighters had been destroyed by a single Rebel spy.

The Rebel had also managed to break into Termo's private quarters and steal two holotapes. There was no telling what the Rebels might do with the stolen tapes. The second tape was especially damaging, as it described the Empire's plan to use contaminated bacta as a weapon. It also detailed hyperspace experiments that were to be conducted on Delrakkin.

Termo was concerned because Grand Moff Tarkin (killed with the destruction of the Death Star) had trusted Captain Skeezer with such secret plans. *Why didn't Tarkin tell me?* Termo wondered. This troubled Termo even more than Captain Skeezer's failure to return from the Yavin system.

Termo recalled the last words Grand Moff Tarkin uttered on the second holotape: *"Although it sounds unlikely, it is possible that the Death Star requires your aid. After you attack Delrakkin, Admiral Termo, you are to travel to the Yavin system and locate the Death Star."*

Delrakkin had been attacked, but not destroyed. Although the Death Star was gone, Admiral Termo brought the *Liquidator* to the Yavin system to follow Grand Moff Tarkin's final command. Termo would find the cause of the Death Star's destruction and avenge Grand Moff Tarkin's death.

Tarkin had recorded a third holotape. After Admiral Termo had played the first two holotapes, he had suspected the third might be the most important of all. Instead of returning it to the safe, Termo had placed it in his breast pocket. When he received an order to play the tape, he would be ready.

Termo turned to Communications Officer Tix. "Is there any signal from the Death Star?" Termo asked, already knowing the answer.

"No, sir," Tix replied.

"Do any of the planets in this system support life?" Termo inquired.

Tix consulted a large monitor, then answered, "No, sir. But three of Yavin's moons are capable of supporting life."

"Which is the nearest of the three?" Termo asked.

"Yavin Eight, sir."

"Then proceed to Yavin Eight," Termo ordered. "Launch the probes for the other moons!"

After leaving Delrakkin, the *Millennium Falcon* blasted into hyperspace with a newly acquired X-wing starfighter secured to its lower hull. Princess Leia Organa and Luke Skywalker sat behind Han Solo and Chewbacca in the cockpit. The droids were in the *Falcon*'s central hold area. They all hoped to reach Yavin Four before the *Liquidator* could locate the Rebel base.

After a long silence, Luke turned to Leia. "Do you really think the Empire might be able to control access to hyperspace?" Luke asked.

"Consider what Grand Moff Tarkin said on the holotape, Luke," Leia answered. "The *Liquidator* attempted to destroy Delrakkin City. The Death Star was prepared to finish off any survivors with contaminated bacta. The Empire was actually willing to neutralize Imperial citizens, just so Grand Moff Tarkin could conduct secret tests."

"But Tarkin is dead!" Luke pointed out.

"Yes, but the Emperor is still alive," Leia explained. "If Palpatine allowed the *Liquidator* to attack Delrakkin, he must believe the hyperspace experiments will work."

"Speaking of hyperspace," Han Solo interrupted, "we're about to come out!" The *Millennium Falcon* shuddered as it slowed to sublight speed and the gas-giant planet Yavin came into view.

A blinking warning light caught Chewbacca's attention. The Wookiee snarled as he adjusted a small computer monitor.

"What's Chewbacca doing?" Leia asked.

"He's spotted another ship on our sensor screen," Solo answered as he glanced at Chewbacca's monitor. "Looks like a Star Destroyer is orbiting Yavin Eight."

"Yavin Eight?" Luke exclaimed. "But that's so far from our present position! How could you know the Star Destroyer's exact location for certain?"

"Don't underestimate the *Falcon*, Luke," Solo retorted. "We've got a top-of-the line sensor suite system onboard. We can detect other ships long before they know we're around."

"I thought it was illegal for freighters to have such long-range sensors," Leia stated.

"*Illegal*? Really? Oh, no!" Solo gasped as if he were genuinely surprised. He turned to his copilot. "Did *you* know it was illegal, Chewie? I hope you kept the *receipt* for our sensor system. Maybe we could get a *refund*!"

The Wookiee replied to Solo's sarcasm with roaring laughter.

Leia shook her head. "Forget I mentioned it, Han," she said. "We're in luck. The Star Destroyer hasn't located the Rebel base yet. Can we get back to Yavin Four without drawing the *Liquidator*'s atttention?"

"No problem," Solo answered as the *Millennium Falcon* launched forward. "We're well out of range of any Imperial scanners. All we have to do is —"

Solo's words were interrupted by a flash of light speeding past the *Falcon*.

"What was *that*?" Leia shouted.

"Looks like some kind of an Imperial probe," Solo answered as he adjusted the controls. "It's on a direct course for Yavin Four."

"We have to stop that probe!" Leia stated.

"I'm going to the lower gunport," Luke said as he scrambled out of his seat.

"Punch it, Chewie!" Solo ordered.

CHAPTER TWO

Yavin Eight filled the *Liquidator*'s viewport. The Star Destroyer had deployed a planetary assault team onto the mountainous moon, searching for any signs of Rebel activity.

Admiral Termo looked away from the viewport and turned to Officer Tix. "What's the report from the surface?" Termo asked.

"Rocky terrain with rodentlike life, sir," Tix answered. "No sign of the Rebellion so far, but we still have a lot of ground to cover."

"We have the entire Yavin *system* to cover, Officer Tix," Termo said. "We'd best move on. Leave the primary assault team on Yavin Eight while we sweep the system with the *Liquidator*. Have the probes reached the other moons?"

Tix glanced at another console. "The Yavin Thirteen probe has landed." Tix tapped at a keyboard and new figures appeared on his screen. "The Yavin Four probe is still in transit, and will arrive shortly. If the Rebels are on Yavin Thirteen, they're heavily concealed, sir."

"Hmmm," Termo mumbled. "Take us out to Yavin Thirteen. We need to be certain."

Tix looked up at Admiral Termo. The commanding officer of the Imperial Star Destroyer *Liquidator* was biting his fingernails.

The *Millennium Falcon* tore through space, racing after the Imperial probe.

"We're almost in range, Luke," Solo spoke into the *Falcon*'s comm.

"I'm ready," Luke answered from his gunport. He adjusted the sights on the quad laser cannon. "I'm getting a visual on the probe." From the gunport, the probe resembled a sleek missile with a pointed, dart-like nosecone.

"Okay, kid," Solo urged, "on my mark —"

"Wait!" Leia shouted, startling Solo. "If Luke misses, the probe might signal the *Liquidator*!"

"I've already got that figured out, Your Observedness — we *won't* miss," Solo replied as he reached for a black button. "Okay, Luke," Solo muttered. "On 'three.' One . . . two . . . *three!*"

At the exact moment Luke fired the laser cannon at the Imperial probe, Solo launched a concussion missile at the same target. A split second later the probe exploded in a bright burst of energy.

"Nice job, Luke!" Solo said into the comm. "Come on back to the cockpit." Solo glanced over his shoulder at Leia. "Pretty smart, huh?"

"Maybe not," Leia answered. "Now that there's no chance for the probe to report back to the *Liquidator*, Admiral Termo will be suspicious when he doesn't receive a signal from Yavin Four."

"Termo will get a signal," Solo assured her. "We'll send a fake transmission saying Yavin Four is clear. That should make the *Liquidator* pass us by."

Before Leia could question Solo's logic, Luke entered the cockpit and asked, "Why did you waste a concussion missile, Han? You *know* I could have shot that probe with my eyes closed!"

Solo chuckled. "And let you have all the fun? You're dreaming!"

The *Falcon* swung hard to the starboard side and Yavin Four came into view. "Buckle up, everybody," Solo commanded. "We'll be landing in a few minutes."

CHAPTER THREE

Imperial Captain Skeezer sat in his white plastic cell on Yavin Four. As best as Skeezer could figure, he had been in his cell for several days. He had not said a word since his experience in the operating room.

In the operating room, a Rebel doctor named Solo had told Skeezer he had been injured during his capture. According to Solo, the injuries required placing Skeezer in a tank filled with bacta from the Death Star. Skeezer had panicked, telling the doctor that the Death Star's bacta was contaminated. Then a Wookiee had entered the operating room and Skeezer had fainted.

When Skeezer had awakened, he was in this cell. He had not been injured at all. Now he realized the Rebels had lied about having bacta from the Death Star. They had tricked him into revealing what he knew of the poisoned cargo.

Although the Rebels might have lied about removing bacta from the Death Star, Skeezer believed they were telling the truth about the destruction of the massive space station. There were two perfectly good reasons for Skeezer's belief: the Death Star had never arrived at Delrakkin, and Yavin Four was still very much in one piece.

Skeezer knew the Rebels would probably pursue the truth about the contaminated bacta. From Thyferra to Delrakkin, he had left a well-covered trail, and he doubted the Rebels would find anything. Still, Skeezer felt well enough to look into the matter himself.

Time to escape, Skeezer thought.

Captain Skeezer fell to the white plastic floor of his cell. He clutched his stomach and groaned loudly.

Three Rebel guards entered Skeezer's cell. "Stand up!" one of the guards commanded.

"I . . . I can't!" Skeezer wheezed through clenched teeth. "I'm sick! I think my food was p-p-poisoned!" Drool fell from Skeezer's lips onto the floor.

Two guards stepped over to the fallen Imperial captain while the third guard remained standing in the doorway. The two guards took hold of Skeezer and lifted him off the floor.

As Skeezer was raised to his feet, he swung his elbow hard into one guard and grabbed the other guard's holstered blaster. In the doorway, the third guard drew his own blaster but was too late. Skeezer fired and the third guard fell backward to the floor. Skeezer twisted sharply, fired twice more, and the other guards went down.

Skeezer checked the still-smoking blaster. It had been set to stun. The three guards would live. The only reason Skeezer did not finish them off was because he didn't want to waste any ammunition.

Skeezer grabbed the other guards' weapons and ran from the cell. He was making his way down a dim corridor when he recognized the scent of engine fuel. As he moved forward, the scent became stronger.

In seconds, Skeezer located the Rebels' hangar. Only a few small fighter craft were visible in the darkness, but they all appeared to be under repair. None of the crafts looked ready for flight. Skeezer stuck to the shadows as he moved across the hangar, heading for the wide doorway.

Outside the hangar, the daylight nearly blinded Captain Skeezer. Squinting, he saw a large group of Rebel technicians and repair droids working on a Gallofree Yards Medium Transport. The transport was too large to fit inside the hangar, which explained why the Rebels worked on it in the open air. Fortunately for Skeezer, the Rebels were too busy with the repairs to notice him.

Captain Skeezer kept close to the ancient temple, moving behind some low shrubs. As he rounded an outside corner of the temple, Skeezer looked up to see another large ship. The Imperial captain's heart skipped a beat.

It was his Carrack cruiser. . . . and it had been completely repaired.

"Oh, dear," Threepio exclaimed as the *Millennium Falcon* angled sharply, descending through the atmosphere of Yavin Four. "I really *do* hate space travel!"

Braced against the wall of the central hold area, Artoo responded to Threepio's comment with a flurry of electronic chirps and whistles.

"Don't call *me* gravity bait, you tottering kettle!" Threepio replied. "You'd hate space travel too if *you* had as many moving parts!"

Q-7N hovered before Threepio's face and asked, "Do you think anyone would mind if I flew to the cockpit? I spent several centuries on Yavin Four, but I've never seen it from space!"

"If anyone minds," Threepio considered, "I'm sure they'll tell you."

Q-7N flew through the narrow passageway to the cockpit. He stopped just to the side of Luke Skywalker's head. Luke turned, surprised, to the small floating droid. Luke smiled and said, "Well hello, Q-7N."

"Hello, Master Luke," Q-7N whispered. "I hope I'm not disturbing anyone, but I hoped I might see Yavin Four from space!"

"By all means," Luke encouraged, extending his hand to the cockpit windows. "Take in the view."

"There's the Rebel base!" Q-7N remarked with great excitement. One of Q-7N's three photoreceptors spotted movement near the ancient temple. "Is that the Carrack cruiser?"

"It sure is," Solo replied. "The repairs must've been completed. Someone is taking it for a test flight."

The Carrack cruiser rose into the air and wobbled slightly before heading toward the *Falcon*.

Chewbacca growled.

"What's that pilot doing?" Leia asked.

"He's heading right for us!" Solo shouted.

Without warning, the Carrack cruiser blasted laser fire at the *Millennium Falcon*. A small explosion rocked the Correllian freighter. Solo gripped the controls, trying to correct his ship's descent.

"The Carrack shot our main deflector shield projector!" Solo yelled. "Who's flying that ship?"

As if in response, the Carrack fired a second blast that struck the *Falcon*'s hull. Chewbacca howled, struggling with the controls as the *Falcon* lurched off course.

"Hang on!" Solo yelled. "It's going to be a rough landing!"

The *Millennium Falcon* swooped low, scraping the

tops of the tall jungle trees. Only Solo and Chewbacca's combined years of flying prevented the bulky freighter from crashing. They landed the ship near the Rebel base, next to the Rebels' medium transport ship.

As soon as the ramp hit the ground, the *Falcon*'s crew and passengers piled out of the damaged ship. A Rebel technician ran from the Gallofree Yards Medium Transport.

"Princess Leia!" the technician called out. "Captain Skeezer escaped in the Carrack cruiser!"

"Skeezer?" Solo said in disbelief. "But how could he —?"

"There's no time for wondering how he escaped!" Leia snapped. "If Skeezer manages to reach the *Liquidator* and alert Termo to our location, we're doomed!"

"Well, the *Falcon*'s not going anywhere without its shields!" Solo scoffed as he looked skywards. The Carrack cruiser was still within sight as it rocketed upwards.

"I don't mean to change the subject," said the Rebel technician, looking at the X-wing attached to the bottom hull of the *Falcon*, "but I would have sworn you left Yavin Four with a Y-wing!"

Leia shot a glance at the X-wing and the other Y-wing and A-wing starfighters nearby. Then she turned to her friends. "Of course! One of us can go after that Carrack immediately!"

MISSION BRIEFING

Before you proceed, you must consult the Mission Guide for the rules of the STAR WARS MISSIONS. You must follow these rules at all times.

This is a Rebel mission.

Imperial Captain Skeezer has escaped in his repaired Carrack cruiser. If Skeezer contacts the Imperial Star Destroyer *Liquidator*, he will reveal the location of the Rebel base to Admiral Termo. The Rebel Alliance lost most of their ships in the battle of Yavin (against the Death Star), and the Rebels are not ready to defend themselves against an attack from an Imperial Star Destroyer. You must prevent Captain Skeezer from reaching the *Liquidator*.

The *Liquidator* is in the Yavin system searching for the cause of the Death Star's destruction. It will not leave until it searches every planet and moon. If the Rebels attempt to escape from Yavin Four, they will probably be attacked by the *Liquidator*. You must prevent the *Liquidator* from reaching Yavin Four.

You start this Mission with your MP total from your previous Mission.

Choose your character. You can take no more than four weapons (including a blaster rifle and a laser pistol), and one vehicle (which must be a starfighter). You can use Power twice in this Mission.

May the Force be with you.

YOUR MISSION: DESTROY THE LIQUIDATOR

"I'll fly the starfighter," you volunteer. There isn't time for any arguments. Running to the vehicle, you clamber up to the cockpit canopy. You pull your helmet over your head and are about to lower the canopy when Q-7N shoots in beside you.

"The others agree I should go with you!" the small flying droid declares.

"Then welcome aboard," you reply as the canopy seals shut. The Rebel technician gives you a thumbs-up signal and you push the throttle. The starfighter lifts off the ground and fires into the sky.

The Carrack cruiser is no longer in sight. "I'll need more speed to catch up with Skeezer," you tell Q-7N.

To increase engine power: Choose your vehicle. (This will be your vehicle for the entire Mission.) Add your skill# to your vehicle's speed# for your confront#. Roll the 6-dice to divert power from your weapons to your engine.

> *If your confront# is equal to or more than your roll#*, add the difference to your MP total. You have caught up with the Carrack and you may proceed.

> *If your confront# is less than your roll#*, subtract the difference from your MP total and repeat this confront until you have caught up with the Carrack.

The Carrack cruiser comes into view. You relay power back to your deflector shields and push the throttle forward.

"The Carrack is heavily armored," you point out. "Unless I can get a clear shot at the power generators, it won't be easy to stop Skeezer."

"Are you certain Captain Skeezer knows about the *Liquidator*'s location?" Q-7N asks.

You check your nav computer. "Well, he's not heading for any standard hyperspace jump point. According to Grand Moff Tarkin's second holotape, Captain Skeezer seemed to know more than Admiral Termo. If Skeezer knew about the bacta plan, he might also know that Termo would bring the *Liquidator* to Yavin."

"Could Captain Skeezer have already contacted the *Liquidator*?" the droid wonders aloud.

"Not yet," you reply. "Piloting the Carrack is a tough job for one person, even for an experienced pilot like Skeezer. He'd have to take his hands off the controls to transmit a signal."

Q-7N adjusts one photoreceptor to a telescopic setting, focusing on the round radio dish atop the fleeing cruiser. "It looks like the Rebel technicians repaired the Carrack's sensor arrays. Unless you can hit the cruiser's power generators, I suggest you try shooting out the sensor dish. That way, Captain Skeezer won't be able to send any signal."

"It's almost a shame that we have to destroy our technicians' repair job!" you comment as you push the starfighter to its fastest sublight speed. In seconds, the Carrack is within firing range. Your fingers tense back on the triggers for the starfighter's laser cannons.

You must destroy the Carrack cruiser's sensor dish.

To shoot the sensor dish: Your vehicle's weaponry# + your weaponry#, is your confront#. Roll the 12-dice to blow the sensor dish into space dust.

If your confront# is equal to or more than your roll#, add the difference +3 to your MP total and proceed.

If your confront# is lower than your roll#, subtract the difference from your MP total. Now double your confront# for your new confront#. Roll the 12-dice again to destroy the sensor dish.

> *If your new confront# is equal to or more than your roll#,* add the difference to your MP total and proceed.

> *If your new confront# is less than your roll#,* subtract the difference from your MP total. Repeat this confront with your new confront# until you have destroyed the sensor dish. Once you have destroyed the sensor dish, you may proceed.

Sparks fly from the top of the Carrack, illuminating the wreckage of the mangled sensor dish. As if in response, the Carrack turns sharply off course, plunging away into space.

"If Skeezer didn't know we were after him, he knows it now!" you declare. "He's switched to an evasive flight path."

Laser fire blasts from the rear of the Carrack and nearly hits your starfighter.

"Skeezer's shooting at us!" Q-7N yelps.

"The Carrack must have an automatic defense system," you realize as you dodge another burst of fire. "I've got to knock out that cannon!"

To destroy the Carrack's aft cannon: Your vehicle's weaponry# +3 is your confront#. Roll the 12-dice to fire at the Carrack's cannon.

If your confront# is equal to or more than your roll#, you're right on target. Add the difference +4 to your MP total and proceed.

If your confront# is lower than your roll#, subtract the difference from your MP total. Now add +3 to your confront# for your new confront#. Roll the 12-dice again to shoot the Carrack's cannon.

If your new confront# is equal to or more than your roll#, add the difference to your MP total and proceed.

If your new confront# is less than your roll#, subtract the difference from your MP total. Repeat this confront with the same confront# until you have destroyed the Carrack's cannon. Then you may proceed.

Despite the Carrack cruiser's length and bulk, it steers into a tight arc, then loops back. The oncoming Carrack appears to grow larger as it races toward you.

"That doesn't look very evasive to me," Q-7N whispers.

"He's going to ram us!" you shout as you pull back on the controls.

You must avoid the cruiser. You can do this by either increasing your speed or changing your direction

To increase your speed: Your skill# + your vehicle's speed# is the confront#. Roll the 6-dice to speed your way out of this one.

If your confront# is equal to or more than your roll#, add the difference to your MP total. You speed out of the Carrack cruiser's way. Now you must loop around for an attack.

If your confront# is less than your roll#, subtract the difference from your MP total. You are still in the cruiser's path. You must choose again whether to increase your speed or change direction (below).

To change direction: Add your skill# to your vehicle's stealth# for your confront#. Roll the 6-dice to dodge the oncoming cruiser.

If your confront# is equal to or more than your roll#, add the difference to your MP total. You have steered into a tight loop and can proceed.

If your confront# is less than your roll#, subtract the difference from your MP total. You are still in the Carrack's path. You must choose again whether to change direction or increase your speed (above.)

The engines whine as you strain your ship out of the maneuvered loop. You end up behind the Carrack.

"Don't let him out of your sight!" Q-7N shouts.

"I'm on him," you counter, increasing the throttle.

"Can't we go any faster?" Q-7N inquires.

"The way Skeezer's flying that thing, it's all I can do to keep up with him," you insist.

The Carrack swerves, heading for a blurry, nebulous mass. From a great distance, it resembles a giant cloud in outer space.

"What is he flying toward?" Q-7N asks. "It almost looks like some kind of enormous fog bank."

As you speed closer, distant particles come into view, and appear to grow larger as you approach. "That's not a fog bank," you inform the droid. "That's a meteor field!"

"A meteor field?" the droid exclaims with genuine fear in his electronic voice. "I've got a bad feeling about this. Should we continue this pursuit?"

"We only knocked out the Carrack's sensor array, Q-7N," you assert, adjusting power to your forward deflector shields. "We can't risk Skeezer reaching the *Liquidator*!" You follow the Carrack into the meteor field.

Your concentration shifts from the pursuit of the Carrack to avoiding the countless meteors. There's no choice but to activate your targeting computer.

"The meteors are throwing off the targeting system!" you shout. "I can't draw a bead on the Carrack! Skeezer's moving too fast!"

Skeezer pilots the Carrack with nerve-racking skill between the meteors. The chase becomes increasingly difficult. Some of the meteors are gigantic, while others are smaller than your vehicle.

Suddenly, a long, heavy meteor spins up in front of you. You can either dodge or destroy the meteor.

To dodge the meteor: Add your skill# to your vehicle's stealth +3 for your confront#. Roll the 12-dice to swoop clear of the meteor.

If your confront# is equal to or more than your roll#, add the difference +3 to your MP total. It was a close call, but you managed to avoid a head-on collision. You may now proceed.

If your confront# is less than your roll#, subtract the difference from your MP total. You've missed your chance to dodge the meteor, and now you must attempt to destroy it (below).

To destroy the meteor: Your vehicle's weaponry# + your weaponry# +1 is your confront#. Roll the 12-dice to fire a proton torpedo at the meteor.

If your confront# is equal to or more than your roll#, add the difference +4 to your MP total. The meteor explodes into a million fragments. You may now proceed.

If your confront# is lower than your roll#, subtract the difference from your MP total. Now add +3 to your confront# for your new confront#. You will now be using laser cannon. Roll the 12-dice again to destroy the meteor.

If your new confront# is equal to or more than your roll#, add the difference to your MP total and proceed.

If your new confront# is less than your roll#, subtract the difference from your MP total. Repeat this confront with your new confront# until you have destroyed the meteor. After it is vaporized, you may proceed.

A larger meteor passes between you and the Carrack. Quickly calculating your options, you realize you could lose the Carrack if you try dodging this meteor. You must destroy it.

To destroy the meteor: Add your skill# to your vehicle's weaponry# +1 for your confront#. Roll the 12-dice to fire a proton torpedo straight into the massive galactic rock.

> *If your confront# is equal to or more than your roll#,* add the difference to your MP total and proceed.

> *If your confront# is less than your roll#,* subtract the difference from your MP total and repeat this confront until you have destroyed the large meteor. Once you have blown it away, you may proceed.

Nice work! Add 35 MP to your MP total (55 MP for Advanced Level players).

You blink as your starfighter soars through the debris of the exploded meteor.

"I've lost sight of the Carrack!" you shout in frustration as you neatly avoid another collision.

"There it is!" Q-7N calls out. "Thirty degrees port, just beyond that egg-shaped meteor."

"I see it," you confirm, following the droid's directions.

You adjust your controls, accelerating after the Carrack. The cruiser turns hard, speeding out between a cluster of small meteors and into clear space.

"The Carrack's starboard power generator is in my sights," you shout, reaching for the triggers of your laser cannons.

To shoot the Carrack cruiser's starboard power generator: Add your weaponry# to your vehicle's weaponry# +2 for your confront#. Roll the 12-dice to fire your laser cannons at the Carrack's power generator.

> *If your confront# is equal to or more than your roll#,* add the difference +4 to your MP total. The starboard power generator erupts in a great flash, and you may proceed.

> *If your confront# is lower than your roll#,* subtract the difference from your MP total. Now add +5 to your confront# for your new confront#. Roll the 12-dice again to shoot the generator.

>> *If your new confront# is equal to or more than your roll#,* you may proceed.

>> *If your new confront# is less than your roll#,* subtract the difference from your MP total. Repeat this confront with your new confront# until you have destroyed the generator. After the generator explodes, you may proceed.

The Imperial cruiser shudders against the blast, and an electrical surge sweeps over the Carrack's hull.

"I think we just knocked out the power to its hyperdrive

system," you yell. "Skeezer won't be able to escape to hyperspace now!"

The Carrack swings into a tight loop, coming up fast and nearly clipping the nose of your ship. You turn hard in pursuit of the Carrack.

A moon comes into view. "That's Yavin Eight," you tell the droid. "Skeezer is heading right for it! Looks like he's going to try an emergency landing!"

"Is there any sign of the *Liquidator*?" Q-7N asks.

"There's nothing on my sensor screens," you relay. "Maybe the Star Destroyer moved on to another moon." A warning light flashes on your controls. "Hang on! My sensors are picking up something up ahead."

"Could it be more Imperials?" asks the droid.

"Whatever it was, it's gone. I'm only receiving static."

The Carrack descends to the mountains of Yavin Eight. Following closely, you pursue the battered cruiser into a narrow ravine. For an instant, you lose sight of the Carrack as it steers around an immense stone column. As you tear around the column, a huge explosion erupts against the side of the ravine. You pull back hard, rising above the explosion.

"What happened?" Q-7N yelps. "Did the Carrack crash?"

"I think so, but I didn't see it actually —"

Without warning, you are interrupted by several bursts of laser fire, tearing the air around you. Channeling reserve power to the starfighter's shields, you try skirting out of the ravine.

"The shots came from above!" you shout. Pulling back on the throttle, you rise up from the ravine. At the upper edge of the mountain, you spot a drop ship. "It's an Imperial assault team!"

"Where did they come from?" Q-7N asks.

"From the *Liquidator*, of course," you answer. "Termo must have deployed a temporary garrison. Captain Skeezer used the Carrack's sensors to locate the garrison, then transmitted a frequency jammer. That explains the static I picked up."

Gazing out the cockpit window, Q-7N warns, "We're about to pick up more than static."

From over the mountain, two TIE fighters come shooting toward you. Pushing on the throttle, you dive back into the ravine. The ravine is lined by high towers of solid magma, creating a treacherous obstacle course.

You can evade or combat the two TIE fighters. If you choose to evade, you can do so with or without Power. If you choose to combat, you can fight them all at once or one at a time. Choose now.

To evade the two TIE fighters (using Power)*: Choose your Vehicle Evasion Power. Add your Jedi# to your Power's low-resist# and your vehicle's stealth# for your confront#. Roll the 6-dice to evade the two TIE fighters.

If your confront# is equal to or more than your roll#, add the difference +2 to your MP total. You have outmaneuvered the TIE fighters and can proceed.

If your confront# is lower than your roll#, subtract the difference from your MP total. You were not able to dodge the TIE fighters. Now you must combat both TIE fighters at once (below).

Note: This counts as one of two Power uses you are allowed in this Mission.

To evade the two TIE fighters (without Power): Your vehicle's stealth# + your skill# is your confront#. Roll the 6-dice to fly into a cave.

If your confront# is equal to or more than your roll#, add the difference +3 to your MP total. As you exit the other end of the cave, you hear twin explosions from behind. The TIE fighters are destroyed and you can proceed.

If your confront# is lower than your roll#, subtract the difference from your MP total. The TIE fighters stay on your tail as you exit the cave. You must now combat both of them at once (below).

To combat both TIE fighters at once: Your vehicle's weaponry# +2 is your confront#. Roll the 6-dice to fire a proton torpedo into one TIE fighter, causing it to collide with the other TIE fighter.

If your confront# is equal to or more than your roll#, add the difference +1 to your MP total. The TIE fighters collide and you can proceed.

If your confront# is lower than your roll#, subtract the difference from your MP total. Your proton torpedo has missed and now you must combat one TIE fighter at a time (below).

To combat one TIE fighter at a time: Add your weaponry# to your vehicle's weaponry# +2 for your confront#. Roll the 12-dice to fire your laser cannons at the first TIE fighter.

> *If your confront# is equal to or more than your roll#*, add the difference to your MP total. You may proceed to combat the second TIE fighter, using the same confront equation.

> *If your confront# is less than your roll#*, subtract the difference from your MP total and repeat this confront, adding +2 to your confront# for your new confront#. Once you have defeated the first TIE fighter, repeat this confront to combat the second TIE fighter, using your old confront#. Once you have defeated both ships, you may proceed.

Rising out of the ravine, you scan the mountains, trying to get your bearings.

"Should we look for the Carrack?" Q-7N asks.

"I'm pretty sure Skeezer crashed," you reply. "I'm more worried about those TIE fighters. As soon as the assault team realizes two TIE fighters are missing, the leader will probably launch a beacon and summon the *Liquidator*."

"Maybe you can locate the Imperial base before any beacon can be launched," Q-7N suggests.

"It's worth trying," you agree, bringing your vehicle around in a wide turn.

Minutes later, the small droid bounces with excitement off of your right shoulder. "Look down off your starboard side!" Q-7N directs. "Is that an Imperial camp?"

"It sure is," you acknowledge. An Imperial drop ship sits at the edge of the ravine. Beside the drop ship, two more TIE fighters rest on an immense stone ledge.

"I'm going for the drop ship!" you announce. "I may not be able to destroy it, but I can at least do some heavy damage." You swoop upward, then loop back toward the drop ship.

You must fire at the drop ship. You can use either your laser cannon or a proton torpedo.

To destroy the drop ship with your laser cannon: Add your weaponry# to your vehicle's weaponry# +4 for your confront#. Roll the 12-dice to fire the laser cannon.

If your confront# is equal to or more than your roll#, add the difference +3 to your MP total. You've scored a direct hit and may now proceed.

If your confront# is less than your roll#, subtract the difference from your MP total. You must try again. Add +2 to your confront# for your new confront#. Repeat this confront with the new confront# until you have destroyed the drop ship.

To destroy the drop ship with a proton torpedo: Add your skill# to your vehicle's weaponry# for your confront#. Roll the 12-dice to fire a proton torpedo at the drop ship's forward control area.

If your confront# is equal to or more than your roll#, add 6 MP to your MP total. You've scored a direct hit on the drop ship and may proceed.

If your confront# is lower than your roll#, subtract the difference from your MP total. Now double your confront# for your new confront#. Roll the 12-dice again to fire a second torpedo at the drop ship.

> *If your new confront# is equal to or more than your roll#*, add the difference to your MP total and proceed.

> *If your new confront# is less than your roll#*, subtract the difference from your MP total. You need to conserve proton torpedoes — switch to your laser cannon until you have destroyed the drop ship (above).

The starfighter plunges away from the explosion, diving downward into the ravine. Gazing at the base of the stone ledge, you notice a giant boulder. "That boulder is under the ledge that supports the TIE fighters," you observe. "If I can shoot it with a proton torpedo, I may be able to take out the TIE fighters." Bringing the ship out of the chasm, you arch upward before you return for another pass at the boulder.

"Hurry!" Q-7N shouts. "We've been spotted! Two Imperial pilots are running for the TIE fighters."

The boulder comes into your sights and you pull the trigger.

To destroy the boulder: Your vehicle's weaponry# + your weaponry# is your confront#. Roll the 6-dice to fire a proton torpedo at the boulder.

> *If your confront# is equal to or more than your roll#*, add the difference to your MP total. The boulder shatters, causing the ledge to crumble. The TIE fighters topple into the ravine and explode against the rocks below. You may now proceed.

> *If your confront# is less than your roll#*, subtract the difference from your MP total. The proton torpedo hit the wrong boulder, and the two Imperial pilots managed to reach their TIE fighters. Now you must combat the two TIE fighters, one at a time (below).

To combat one TIE fighter at a time: Add your skill# to your weaponry# + your vehicle's weapon# for your confront#. Roll the 12-dice to fire your laser cannons at the first TIE fighter.

> *If your confront# is equal to or more than your roll#*, add the difference to your MP total. The first TIE fighter goes down in a fiery explosion. You may proceed to combat the second TIE fighter, using the same confront equation. Once you have defeated both TIE fighters, you may proceed.

> *If your confront# is less than your roll#*, subtract the difference from your MP total and repeat this confront, adding +3 to your confront# for your new confront#. Once you have defeated the first TIE fighter, repeat this confront to combat the second TIE fighter using your old confront#.

As you fly over the wreckage of the Imperial campsite, Q-7N directs a photoreceptor toward the ground below. "What are those tracks?" the droid asks. "They look like giant footprints leading away from the campsite."

"That's odd," you remark. "No one has ever described any giant creatures on this moon. We'd better investigate." Flying lower to the ground, you recognize the trail of deep tracks. "Oh, no," you murmur, your voice filled with dread. "Only one thing leaves a trail like that."

In the distance, a tall shadow emerges against the sky. Bringing the X-wing even lower to the ground, you fly toward the shadowy figure.

"What is it?" whispers Q-7N. "Is it some kind of droid?"

"No, Q-7N," you answer. "That's an Imperial All Terrain Armored Transport walker, also called an AT-AT. The Empire uses them for ground assaults."

"Can you destroy it?" the worried droid asks.

"I don't know," you reply. "AT-ATs are heavily armored." As the AT-AT comes into range, the walking vehicle halts. Its "head," the command section, turns to face your direction.

"I think they see us coming!" Q-7N exclaims. As if in confirmation of the droid's words, the AT-AT opens fire at your oncoming ship. You must evade the attack.

To evade the AT-AT attack: Add your skill# to your vehicle's stealth# for your confront#. Roll the 6-dice to fly under the "body" of the gigantic walking vehicle.

If your confront# is equal to or more than your roll#, add the difference +1 to your MP total. The AT-AT is unable to fire at you as the X-wing swoops beneath its hull. You may now proceed.

If your confront# is less than your roll#, subtract the difference from your MP total and repeat this confront until you have evaded the AT-AT.

Looping back to attack, you approach the AT-AT from the side. Pulling on your triggers, you squeeze off several shots at the command section. The laser blasts strike the hull, but barely dent the mechanical menace. "I'll have to aim for one of its knee joints!" you relay to Q-7N.

"Or you can use your grappling hook and bring the AT-AT to its knees," Q-7N points out.

To bring the AT-AT down with your grappling hook: Your skill# + your vehicle's stealth# is your confront#. Roll the 6-dice to trip the behemoth vessel.

If your confront# is equal to or more than your roll#, add the difference to your MP total. You've brought down the AT-AT by tying its legs. You may now proceed.

If your confront# is less than your roll#, subtract the difference from your MP total. You must try again. Repeat this confront until you have toppled the AT-AT.

To shoot the AT-AT: Add your weaponry# to your vehicle's weaponry# +2 for your confront#. Roll the 12-dice to fire a proton torpedo at the round joint on the AT-AT's right front leg.

If your confront# is equal to or more than your roll#, add the difference +4 to your MP total. The AT-AT's right front leg ruptures, causing the behemoth to stumble and crash to the ground. You may now proceed.

If your confront# is lower than your roll#, subtract the difference from your MP total. Now add +2 to your confront# for your new confront#. Roll the 12-dice again to fire another blast, this time at the AT-AT's left front leg joint.

> *If your new confront# is equal to or more than your roll#*, add the difference to your MP total and proceed.

> *If your new confront# is less than your roll#*, subtract the difference from your MP total. Repeat this confront with your new confront# until you have toppled the AT-AT. Once the knee joint is destroyed, you may proceed.

For destroying the AT-AT, add 60 MP to your MP total (75 MP for Advanced Level players).

As the AT-AT crashes against the ground, a flare erupts from its command section. A small missile speeds past your wing, then rises straight up into the sky.

"They fired a distress beacon!" you yell. Pulling back on the throttle, you bring up your ship in pursuit of the missile. "We can't let it reach the *Liquidator*!"

The missile comes into your line of vision and you adjust the settings on your weapons. "This'll be a tricky shot," you admit. "The missile is a small target, and it's on an evasive flight path. My targeting computer can't get a lock on it!"

"Go to manual!" the droid encourages.

The missile blasts through the stratosphere and into space. In seconds, it seems to transform into a small, glowing circle amidst the stars. Fearing what will happen if you lose sight of the missile, you force your eyes wide open. The sound of static bursts from your sensors — you try to block out the noise. Bringing your vehicle up behind the missile, you wait until the Imperial beacon is directly in front of your ship.

To destroy the emergency distress beacon: Add your weaponry# to your vehicle's weaponry# +3 for your confront#. Roll the 12-dice to fire your laser cannons at the tiny missile.

If your confront# is equal to or more than your roll#, add the difference +2 to your MP total. The missile erupts in an almost blinding flash of light. But it may have already transmitted its signal. With this in mind, you may now proceed.

If your confront# is less than your roll#, subtract 7 MP from your MP total. You have missed the missile. Prepare to face the consequences.

Suddenly, the starfighter is enveloped by a bright blue light. The starfighter shudders and lurches hard to one side.

"Now what?" Q-7N cries out.

"We're caught in a tractor beam!" Craning your head back, you gaze outside and above the starfighter. A wedge-shaped vessel blocks out the stars. "It's the *Liquidator*. The beacon transmitted the signal after all."

"Can we escape?" the worried droid whispers.

The controls don't respond. "I'm afraid it doesn't look good, Q-7N," you reply. "They've jammed our ship's systems. But one thing is certain." Reaching to your hip, you unholster your blaster and confirm it carries a full load. "I'm not going without a fight."

"Wait!" Q-7N cautions. "There may be another way out of this." As your ship is drawn into the docking bay of the *Liquidator*, Q-7N whispers a plan. "The Empire is looking for *you*, not some old droid! If you allow yourself to be captured, I can try to rescue you."

"I hope you'll do more than *try*," you reply. "But I guess it's our best chance. Okay, Q-7N. I'm counting on you." You return your blaster to its holster. "So tell me, Q-7N. Have you ever fired a laser cannon before?"

"I beg your pardon?" Q-7N replies.

Worriedly, you tell him your plan.

The tractor beam places you inside the docking bay. It is the same docking bay used for the Empire's fleet of X-wings, the ships used to fake a Rebel attack on Delrakkin. Several damaged X-wings are in sight, all under repair by Imperial work crews. Looking on either side of your ship, you are surrounded by dozens of stormtroopers. They all aim their blasters in the direction of your cockpit.

Checking to make sure Q-7N is tucked down under the control panels, you throw a switch to open the transparisteel canopy. "Here goes nothing," you mumble as the canopy rises.

"Come out with your hands up!" orders an Imperial soldier.

Keeping your hands in clear sight, you slowly extricate

yourself from your vehicle. The stormtroopers keep their weapons trained on you. Stepping down to the docking bay floor, you are approached by a tall officer.

"Greetings," the officer sneers. "Now, will you tell us the location of the Rebel base or should we introduce you to a pain droid?"

Staring the officer in the eye, you sound remarkably bored as you utter, "You won't get anything out of *me*, Admiral Termo."

The admiral's eyes twitch slightly, as if he's trying to figure out what you look like without your flight helmet. "You know my name," the admiral acknowledges, "but I don't believe we've met."

"Not formally," you answer, "but you've got a lousy reputation."

An evil smile crosses Admiral Termo's mouth. "It's not wise to mock me, Rebel scum!" Termo hisses. "I may not know your name, but I know who you are." He gestures to your captured starfighter. "You're probably the spy who stole my holotapes!"

You nod in agreement. "Guilty," you admit. Then in a loud clear voice, you shout, "Now, Q-7N!"

In the cockpit, the droid responds to your command, pushing its full weight against the starfighter triggers. Blaster fire erupts from its laser cannons. The explosion hits a far wall, sending dozens of stormtroopers diving for cover.

Termo raises his arm to shield his eyes from the blast. You seize the opportunity to leap for a nearby doorway.

You know that you cannot fight this many stormtroopers with just your blaster. You must evade the stormtroopers in the docking bay. Choose to evade them with or without Power.

To evade (without Power): Your stealth# +2 is your confront#. Roll the 6-dice to escape through the docking bay door.

If your confront# is equal to or more than your roll#, add the difference to your MP total. You've managed to leap through the doorway and into an empty corridor. You may now proceed.

If your confront# is less than your roll#, subtract the difference from your MP total and repeat this confront until you have passed through the door, and then you may proceed. •

To evade (using Power)*: Choose your Deception or Evasion Power. Add your stealth# and Jedi# to your Power's low-resist# for your confront#. Roll the 6-dice to avoid the nearby stormtroopers.

If your confront# is equal to or more than your roll#, add the difference to your MP total. The stormtroopers cannot see you. You make it to the doorway, then proceed.

If your confront# is lower than your roll#, subtract the difference from your MP total. Repeat this confront until you have escaped the docking bay. After you escape, you may proceed.

Note: This counts as one of two Power uses you are allowed in this Mission.

Racing down the corridor, you ignore the sound of blaster fire from the docking bay behind you. The corridor is empty, but you know the stormtroopers will be coming after you in a matter of seconds. Remembering the layout of the *Liquidator* from the last time you sneaked on board (and stole Termo's two holotapes), you race to a hydrolift and press a button.

Waiting for the arrival of the hydrolift, you cast a glance behind you. Your head rocks back as a small metal object strikes against the front of your helmet.

"Psst!" a voice whispers beside your head.

"Q-7N!" you exclaim. "You nearly made my heart stop! I didn't expect you to come after me so soon."

"Well, you didn't really expect me to stick around that docking bay, did you?" the droid replies. "You should have seen those stormtroopers. They didn't know where to shoot first!"

The hydrolift arrives and you step inside with the droid.

"What will we do now?" Q-7N wonders aloud. "We can't very easily go back the way we came."

"We're going to a weapons storage area," you confide. "We've got to get ahold of a thermal detonator."

The hydrolift stops abruptly. A stormtrooper sentry turns to face you, instantly recognizing your Alliance-issued flightsuit.

You must either bluff your way past the stormtrooper or combat him.

To bluff (without Power): Your charm# +1 is your con-front#. You tell the stormtrooper you are one of the pilots for the Imperial squadron of X-wings. Roll the 6-dice to see if he falls for it.

If your confront# is equal to or more than your roll#, add the difference +2 to your MP total. The stormtrooper falls for your lie. You may procced.

If your confront# is less than your roll#, subtract the dif-ference from your MP total. The stormtrooper sees right through your lie. You must combat him (below).

To bluff (with Power)*: Choose your Deception or Per-suasion Power. Your charm# + your Power's mid-resist# + your Jedi# is your confront#. You tell the stormtrooper you are one of the pilots for the Imperial squadron of X-wings. Roll the 6-dice to see if he falls for it.

If your confront# is equal to or more than your roll#, add the difference +2 to your MP total. The stormtrooper falls for your lie. You may proceed.

If your confront# is less than your roll#, subtract the dif-ference from your MP total. The stormtrooper sees right through your lie. You must combat him (below).

***Note:** This counts as one of two Power uses you are allowed in this Mission.

To combat the trooper: Choose your weapon. Add your weaponry# to your weapon's close-range# for your confront#. Roll the 6-dice to shoot the trooper.

If your confront# is equal to or more than your roll#, add the difference to your MP total. The stormtrooper is knocked out of his Imperial boots by the power of the blast. You may proceed.

If your confront# is less than your roll#, subtract the difference from your MP total and repeat this confront until you have vanquished the stormtrooper. Once he is neutralized, you may proceed.

"The weapons storage area is this way," you tell Q-7N.

"How do you know your way around Star Destroyers?"

"Over the years, a few Imperial pilots have left the Empire to join the Alliance. They've provided a lot of valuable information, even blueprints of Imperial vessels."

You arrive at the door to the weapons storage area. The door is locked.

You must open the door to the weapons storage area. You can either hotwire the lock, blast the door open, kick the door in, or use Power to open the door.

To hotwire the lock: Your skill# +1 is your confront#. Roll the 6-dice to open the door with remarkable ease.

If your confront# is equal to or more than your roll#, add the difference to your MP total. Q-7N compliments you on your ability to unlock virtually any door, and then you proceed.

If your confront# is less than your roll#, subtract the difference from your MP total. The Imperial locksmiths created a door you can't open. You'll have to blast the door open or kick it in (below). Choose before you proceed.

To blast the door open: Choose your weapon. Your weapon's close-range# +1 is your confront#. Roll the 6-dice to blow the door off its hinges.

If your confront# is equal to or more than your roll#, add the difference to your MP total. There's a smoldering metal hole where the door used to be, and you proceed into the room.

If your confront# is less than your roll#, subtract the difference from your MP total and repeat this confront until you have blown the door down.

To kick in the door: Your strength# +1 is your confront#. Roll the 6-dice to get into the storage room.

If your confront# is equal to or more than your roll#, add the difference to your MP total. You're through the door in a matter of seconds.

If your confront# is less than your roll#, subtract the difference from your MP total. You must try again. Either blast the door open (above) or try to kick it in again, using the same confront equation.

To use Power to open the lock*: Choose your Object Movement Power. Your skill# + your Jedi# is your confront#. Roll the 6-dice to get into the storage room.

If your confront# is equal to or more than your roll#, add the difference to your MP total. You push open the door and proceed.

If your confront# is less than your roll#, subtract the difference from your MP total. You must try again. You must either blast the door open or kick it open (above).

*Note: This counts as one of two Power uses you are allowed in this Mission.

As you enter the weapons storage room, a stormtrooper steps from the shadows. "You there!" shouts the trooper. "Stop where you are!"

Choose to dodge the stormtrooper, persuade the stormtrooper you are an Imperial officer, or combat the stormtrooper. If you choose combat, you can either fight hand-to-hand or with a weapon. There are explosive devices in the weapons storage room. Think twice before you choose a weapon.

To dodge the trooper: Your stealth# +1 is your confront#. Roll the 6-dice to evade.

If your confront# is equal to or more than your roll#, add the difference to your MP total. You've made it past the trooper. You may proceed.

If your confront# is less than your roll#, subtract the difference from your MP total. You can't make it past the stormtrooper. You must combat him, either with a weapon or hand-to-hand (below).

To persuade the trooper (with Power)*: Choose your Persuasion Power. Your charm# + your Power's low-resist# + your Jedi# is your confront#. You tell the stormtrooper you are really an Imperial officer disguised as a Rebel. Roll the 6-dice to see if he is stupid enough to believe you.

If your confront# is equal to or more than your roll#, add the difference to your MP total. The stormtrooper believes you. You may procced.

If your confront# is less than your roll#, subtract the difference from your MP total. The stormtrooper sees right through your lie. You must combat him, either with a weapon or hand-to-hand (below).

*Note: This counts as one of two Power uses you are allowed in this Mission.

To persuade the stormtrooper (without Power): Your charm# +2 is your confront#. Roll the 12-dice to tell the stormtrooper that you are really an Imperial officer disguised as a Rebel.

If your confront# is equal to or more than your roll#, add the difference +3 to your MP total. Believing you are his commanding officer, the stormtrooper steps aside. You can take whatever you want.

If your confront# is less than your roll#, subtract the difference from your MP total. The stormtrooper doesn't believe you at all. Now you must fight the storm-trooper by hand-to-hand combat (below).

To fight the stormtrooper hand-to-hand: Add your skill# to your strength# +3 for your confront#. Roll the 12-dice to throw a devastating punch at the stormtrooper.

> *If your confront# is equal to or more than your roll#,* add the difference +1 to your MP total. Your punch lifts the stormtrooper off his feet; his helmet bounces against the ceiling before he drops to the floor. You may now proceed.

> *If your confront# is less than your roll#,* subtract the difference from your MP total. This stormtrooper is too tough for you. You'll have to combat him with a weapon (below).

To combat the stormtrooper with a weapon: Choose your weapon. Add your weaponry# to your weapon's close-range# for your confront#. Roll the 12-dice to combat the trooper.

> *If your confront# is equal to or more than your roll#,* add the difference +3 to your MP total. The storm-trooper slams against the far wall, and you pro-ceed.

> *If your confront# is lower than your roll#,* subtract the difference from your MP total. Now add +2 to your con-front# for your new confront#. Roll the 12-dice again to combat the stormtrooper.

If your new confront# is equal to or more than your roll#, add the difference to your MP total and proceed.

If your new confront# is less than your roll#, subtract the difference from your MP total. Repeat this confront with your new confront# until you have defeated the stormtrooper. Then you may proceed.

Reward yourself 45 MP for defeating the stormtrooper (60 MP for Advanced Level Players).

Going to a shelf, you see several thermal detonators. You find the one you want. The detonator is heavier than it looks, but you manage to place it into your flightsuit's backpack.

"Let's hope nobody shoots me in the back," you mutter.

"Where are we going with that detonator?" Q-7N inquires, following you back into the corridor.

"I'm going to try blowing up the *Liquidator*'s solar ionization reactor," you answer, refering to the massive protuberance at the base of the Star Destroyer. "This ship is heavily shielded on the outside, but it's not protected from an inside attack. A well-placed thermal detonator should destroy the entire ship."

"*The entire ship?*" Q-7N echoes in disbelief as the elevator doors close. "And just where will *we* be when that happens?"

"I picked a thermal detonator with a timing mechanism," you tell the droid. "With any luck, we'll be able to make it to an escape pod before the first explosion."

"Then let's hope we're lucky," Q-7N states as the elevator opens to another corridor.

Running close to the wall, you make your way toward the main control room of the solar ionization reactor.

"I wonder why we haven't run into more stormtroopers?" Q-7N comments.

"I think we left most of them in the docking bay," you reply. "But we've got to move fast before they find us!"

At the entrance to the control room, a menacing droid guards the door. It's taller than you, and both of its arms end in sharp, lethal weapons. Four electronic eyes glow red on its black metal head. The droid turns to face you.

You must gain entrance to the control room. Choose now to evade or combat the droid.

To evade the guard droid (without Power): Add your skill# to your stealth# for your confront#. Roll the 6-dice to slip past the guard droid.

If your confront# is equal to or more than your roll#, add the difference to your MP total. Looking at the spot where you were just standing, the guard droid makes a whirring sound, wondering whether there is something wrong with its photoreceptors. You duck into the control room and proceed.

If your confront# is less than your roll#, subtract the difference from your MP total. You were not able to sneak past the guard droid, and now you must combat it (below).

To evade the guard droid (using Power)*: Choose your Evasion Power. Your stealth# + your Power's mid-resist# + your Jedi# is your confront#. Roll the 12-dice to slip past the guard droid.

> If your confront# is equal to or more than your roll#, add the difference to your MP total. Looking at the spot where you were just standing, the guard droid makes a whirring sound, wondering whether there is something wrong with its photoreceptors. You duck into the control room and proceed.

> If your confront# is less than your roll#, subtract the difference from your MP total. You were not able to sneak past the guard droid. You must combat it (below).

*Note: This counts as one of two Power uses you are allowed in this Mission.

To combat the guard droid: Choose your weapon. Add your weaponry# to your weapon's mid-range# -1 for your confront#. Roll the 6-dice to defend yourself against the guard droid.

> If your confront# is equal to or more than your roll#, add the difference to your MP total. The guard droid explodes into a useless heap of junk.

> If your confront# is less than your roll#, subtract the difference from your MP total and repeat this confront until you have defeated the Imperial guard droid.

Entering the control room, you come upon a bank of computers. Another doorway looks out on the inner core of the solar ionization reactor. A catwalk stretches from the door to the center of the reactor. Q-7N gazes around the control room and asks, "Are you going to set the bomb in here?"

Studying a computer screen, you answer, "I'm afraid not." Pointing out the window, you proclaim, "According to this computer, I'll have to set it off at the end of that catwalk."

Passing through the doorway, you step onto the catwalk. The walls of the reactor core are illuminated with tall, thin lights. It feels as if you are standing within a deep, enormous well. Taking a quick, dizzying look downward, you realize you can't see the bottom of the reactor. A second catwalk is visibly suspended at a lower level, leading to another part of the ship. If you fall into the reactor, you will surely perish.

"Better keep your balance," Q-7N advises.

"No kidding," you reply as you move forward.

At the end of the catwalk, you reach the top of a metal pylon. Removing the thermal detonator from your backpack, you place it on the pylon and set the timer.

"How long do we have?" asks Q-7N.

"Five minutes," you answer. "Not much time, but long enough to find an escape pod and get —"

"Don't move!" orders a distant voice. Looking across the length of the catwalk to the control room, you see Admiral Termo. The admiral stands next to an Imperial commumnications officer and a dozen stormtroopers.

Unholstering your blaster, you aim the weapon at the thermal detonator. "It's too late, Termo — I've planted a thermal detonator! In less than five minutes, this whole ship is going to be one big fireball."

"Then I suggest you deactivate it, you fool," Termo shouts.

"Forget it, Termo!" Bringing the blaster tip dangerously close to the thermal detonator, you warn, "If even one of your stupid stormtroopers tries anything, I'll blow us up."

"You're bluffing!" Termo snarls.

"I think he means it, sir," the communications officer mutters. "If he even touches that detonator the wrong way, we could all perish!"

You turn sadly to the floating droid. "It doesn't look like there's any way out of this one, Q-7N," you whisper. "Sorry I got you into this."

"Wait!" Q-7N replies. "Look down to your right! Didn't you notice the lower catwalk? If you can jump to it, we could still make it out of here!"

"That's got to be an eight-meter fall!" you groan.

"Well, you can't stay on this catwalk forever," Q-7N points out.

To leap from the upper catwalk to the lower catwalk: Add your skill# to your strength# for your confront#. Roll the 12-dice to dive headfirst to the lower catwalk.

If your confront# is equal to or more than your roll#, add 12 MP to your MP total. You land on the lower catwalk, execute a forward roll, and come up standing. You may now proceed.

If your confront# is less than your roll#, subtract the difference from your MP total. You're about to miss the lower catwalk — you reach out and grab the edge. Now you must pull yourself up (below).

To pull yourself up: Your strength# +1 is your confront#. Roll the 6-dice to pull yourself onto the lower catwalk.

If your confront# is equal to or more than your roll#, you've made it. Add 5 MP to your MP total. Take a deep breath — and proceed.

If your confront# is less than your roll#, subtract the difference from your MP total. You are still hanging on. Try again to pull yourself up, using the same confront equation.

Laser bolts rip into the flooring near your feet, missing you by millimeters. The stormtroopers are trying to shoot you from above.

"Don't shoot the Rebel!" Termo shouts from the control room, reprimanding the stormtroopers. "He's the only one who can deactivate the thermal detonator."

Q-7N hovers before you, darting toward the end of the lower catwalk. The droid flies to an open hatch. "This way!" Q-7N calls out.

Racing after the droid, you slip through the hatch. "We've got about four minutes before the bomb detonates," you remark, following the droid into a cool corridor. "From what I remember about the design of Star Destroyers, there should be an escape pod bay somewhere up ahead."

You turn right at the end of the corridor, then left. With barely two minutes to spare, you pass a hydrolift, then arrive upon two emergency hatches, each leading to an escape pod. "Which one should we take?" Q-7N asks.

"This one's closer!" you reply, placing your hand on a switch to open the nearest escape pod.

The hatch remains closed, but a light flashes from a small console and a computerized voice proclaims, "Enter your personal identification code for access to the lifepod!"

"You want identification?" you shout, drawing your blaster. "How's this for an ID?"

You can either kick open the door, hotwire it, or blast it open.

To kick in the door: Your strength# +1 is your confront#. Roll the 6-dice to get into the lifepod.

> *If your confront# is equal to or more than your roll#,* add the difference to your MP total. You've made it into the lifepod.

> *If your confront# is less than your roll #,* subtract the difference from your MP total. You must try again. Either blast the door open (below) or try to kick it in again, using the same confront equation.

To hotwire the lock: Your skill# +1 is your confront#. Roll the 6-dice to escape.

> *If your confront# is equal to or more than your roll#,* add the difference to your MP total. The lock is open. You push open the door and proceed.

If your confront# is less than your roll#, subtract the difference from your MP total. You must try again. You can either try to hotwire the lock again (using the same confront equation), try to kick in the door (above), or blast it open (below).

To blast open the door: Choose your weapon. Add your weaponry# to your weapon's close-range# for your confront#. Roll the 6-dice to destroy the computer access panel.

If your confront# is equal to or more than your roll#, add the difference +2 to your MP total. The emergency door slides open, and you proceed.

If your confront# is less than your roll#, subtract the difference from your MP total and repeat this confront until you have destroyed the computer access panel.

Just as you are about to enter the lifepod, the sound of blaster fire fills the corridor. The shot narrowly misses you, tearing through your flightsuit's backpack. You whirl sideways, looking down the length of the corridor to see Admiral Termo leaping out of the hydrolift. He holds a blaster rifle in his hands.

"You could have taken the lift," Termo taunts. "Now drop your weapon, or the next shot will kill you." The admiral is out of breath from his swift pursuit, but his rifle doesn't waver. The communications officer and a stormtrooper edge out of the elevator, their blasters drawn.

"Okay, Termo," you answer. "I'm going to put my blaster down on the floor."

"Do it slowly!" Termo yells. "Then tell us how to deactivate the detonator."

Bending down, you lower your blaster toward the floor.

"You're not *really* surrendering?" Q-7N whispers.

"Get in the escape pod and brace yourself," you whisper in return, keeping your grip on the blaster. Q-7N glides into the pod.

"Hurry!" Termo screams.

Raising your arm rapidly, you aim at the startled admiral and snarl, "You forgot to say 'please'!"

To combat Admiral Termo: Choose your weapon. Add your weaponry# to your weapon's mid-range# for your confront#. Roll the 12-dice to shoot the blaster rifle right out of his hands.

> *If your confront# is equal to or more than your roll#,* add 8 MP to your MP total. The scorched rifle flies from Termo's hands, and you proceed.

> *If your confront# is less than your roll#,* subtract the difference from your MP total and repeat this confront, adding +2 to your confront# for your new confront#. Once you have knocked the weapon out of Termo's hands, you may proceed.

Leaping into the escape pod, you throw a switch and the door slides shut. An explosive hiss fills the small chamber as the pod is released and jettisoned from the *Liquidator*.

Casting a quick glance out the pod's window, the Star Destroyer appears to grow smaller as the pod falls in the direction of Yavin's eighth moon.

"Don't look!" Q-7N cautions. "The explosion could blind you."

Following the wise droid's hasty advice, you turn your head from the window and close your eyes. Seconds later, the pod is filled by an incredibly bright flash, followed by the sound of a massive explosion. The resulting shock wave hits the pod, sending it spiraling faster toward Yavin Eight.

Seconds later, the light dims and you dare to look out the window. Twinkling sparks are all that remain of the *Liquidator*.

Turning to Q-7N, you exclaim, "We did it."

"I can't believe it," the droid answers, "but I guess we did."

Reaching to a small console, you tap a series of coordinates into a computer. "I'm transmitting a subspace signal to alert the Alliance that we're still alive."

Within minutes, the escape pod reaches the surface of Yavin Eight and lands on a rocky plateau. The pod's door slides open and you step out onto the moon. Q-7N flies out after you. "I never thought I'd be happy to see this moon again," the droid comments, then aims a photoreceptor at some nearby cliffs. Thick, black smoke rises from beyond the cliffs. "What do you think is causing all that smoke?" Q-7N asks.

Following the droid's gaze, you reply, "I don't know, but let's hope it's not —"

Your words are interrupted by a powerful blast, throwing you away from the escape pod. Rolling to your feet, you stand to see smoke rising from the ruined launcher. Beyond the launcher, an Imperial captain stands with a blaster rifle aimed at you.

"Captain Skeezer!" Q-7N declares. "He's alive!"

Skeezer's uniform is covered with dirt and grime. "You forced me to crash-land the Carrack on this lousy moon," Skeezer bellows. "Now it's payback time!"

You must fight Captain Skeezer. You can choose to combat with a weapon or with your bare fists.

To combat Captain Skeezer with a weapon: Choose your weapon. Add your weaponry# to your weapon's mid-range# for your confront#. Roll the 6-dice to combat Skeezer.

If your confront# is equal to or more than your roll#, add the difference to your MP total. Unfortunately for Captain Skeezer, you were too fast for him. He collapses to the ground, and you proceed.

If your confront# is lower than your roll#, subtract the difference from your MP total. Skeezer has knocked your weapon away. Now you must fight him hand-to-hand (below).

To combat Captain Skeezer hand-to-hand: Add your skill# to your strength# for your confront#. Roll the 6-dice to throw an uppercut to Skeezer's ugly jaw.

If your confront# is equal to or more than your roll#, add the difference to your MP total. You unleash your rage against the Empire in a single blow to Captain Skeezer. He falls to the ground and you proceed.

If your confront# is less than your roll#, subtract the difference from your MP total and repeat this confront until you have punched out Captain Skeezer, then proceed.

Walking over to Skeezer's fallen body, you bend down to check his pulse.

"Is he neutralized?" Q-7N asks.

"I'm afraid so," you reply. "I'd hoped to capture him alive. I suspect Skeezer knew more about the Empire's plan to control access to hyperspace. Now we may never learn the whole truth."

The noise of a familiar starship engine fills the air. Gazing upward, you see the *Millennium Falcon* fly across the sky.

"What luck!" Q-7N exclaims with glee. "Our friends received our signal and located us!"

"They've also repaired the *Falcon*," you observe. Throwing a smile at the small, flying droid, you beckon, "Come on, pal. We're going home!"

THE AFTER-MISSION

The escape pod that landed on Yavin Eight was not the only vessel to survive the destruction of the *Liquidator*. One other escape pod managed to jettison before the single thermal detonator blew up the Imperial Star Destroyer.

The other escape pod contained two passengers, both human. At first, they considered themselves lucky to be alive. But as they gazed outside the pod's small, round window, they realized they might not be so lucky after all. Instead of falling toward Yavin's eighth moon, the other escape pod was flung into the opposite direction, toward the farthest reaches of deep space. Furthermore, the explosion that destroyed the *Liquidator* also wreaked havoc on the pod's navigational system.

"What do you mean, you don't know how to fix the computer?" Admiral Termo asked.

"I'm sorry, sir," Communications Officer Tix answered. "Without the proper tools, I'm afraid there's very little I can do."

Termo reached into his breast pocket and retrieved Tarkin's third holotape. "I don't suppose there's a holoprojector in this contraption," Termo muttered.

"No, sir," Tix replied.

"Oh, well," Termo said as he placed the unplayed holotape back in his pocket. "It looks like we're in for a long ride."

Back on Yavin Four, the *Millennium Falcon*'s return was greeted with great fanfare. A large crowd gathered outside the Rebel base, cheering for their heroes. General

Dodonna stood before the crowd, leading them in joyous applause.

Princess Leia and Luke Skywalker were the first to step out of the *Falcon*. The crowd was so loud, Luke had to shout to be heard by Leia. "Quite a welcoming committee we've got here, isn't it, Princess?"

"Enjoy it while you can, Luke," answered Leia. "Even though the *Liquidator* is gone, we still have plenty of work to do."

Chewbacca and Han Solo followed Leia and Luke. Chewbacca, basking in the adoration of the cheering Rebels, let loose with a mighty roar. The crowd responded to the Wookiee with even louder cheers.

"I never thought I'd say this, Chewie," Solo admitted, "but it sure feels good to be back on Yavin Four!"

Artoo-Detoo rolled down the *Falcon*'s ramp, beeping and whistling. See-Threepio, following close beside his astromech counterpart, halted on the ramp. "That's funny," Threepio commented. "Where's Q-7N?" Threepio turned to see the small floating droid hovering cautiously at the top of the ramp.

"What's wrong, Q-7N?" Threepio asked.

"Why are all the other Rebels yelling at us?" Q-7N exclaimed.

Artoo rotated his photoreceptor to Q-7N and emitted a series of beeps.

"I agree, Artoo," Threepio complied. "It *is* a bizarre custom!" Turning back to the floating droid, Threepio said, "As ridiculous as this may sound, Q-7N, the Rebels are yelling because they're *happy!*"

"How strange," sighed Q-7N. "I don't suppose I'll ever really understand humans!"

The celebration lasted late into the night. But all too soon, Princess Leia would be proved correct. The battle against the Empire was far from over.

NEXT MISSION: THE HUNT FOR HAN SOLO